Adapted from the Universal film *The Wolf Man*
by Justine Korman

Illustrated by Art Ruiz

Western Publishing Company, Inc., Racine, Wisconsin 53404

Contents

CHAPTER 1
Gypsies

A sleek limousine sped through the hilly countryside. Damp autumn leaves spun up around the car as it made its way along a twisting road. A cool wind rustled through the trees that lined the road, bringing a chilly hint of the bitter winter winds to come.

This far country, Wales, was a land of myths and legends. Visitors traveling through the mysterious wooded landscape often imagined they saw the very dragons and monsters that were talked about at local inns and lodges.

The limousine's passenger, Larry Talbot, paid little attention to the scenery that flashed by the car windows, however. Larry had spent many days traveling from California to England, then riding the train west to Wales. He had been met at the railroad station just hours before by his father's driver. Now they were hurrying home to Talbot Castle in the middle of Wales. Although Larry had come as quickly as possible, he had still missed the

1

funeral of his older brother, John.

Larry thought of his father and his brother. His childhood had been spent in the cold, stone castle, trying to stay out of everyone's way. John had been the favorite. He was the first son and heir, and had been named after his father. Larry had always felt useless around his brother, who seemed so much better at everything than he was. So Larry had left Wales as soon as he was old enough to be on his own. Secretly he had hoped to return someday in triumph, rich and successful on his own, not just as Sir John Talbot's son. Larry never imagined that a tragic hunting accident would bring him back to the twisting roads of his homeland. And he still could not believe his brother, John, was dead.

Larry's heart froze with dread as the car slowed down to enter the narrow streets of the tiny village below Talbot Castle. Time had not touched this place. The cobbled streets, cramped shops, and steepled church were exactly the same. The car began to make the last part of its journey, up a steep mountain. Finally it rolled through the wrought-iron gates of the castle and onto the gravel driveway past a sprawling lawn.

The limousine came to a stop before the arched doorway of the impressive stone building, with its small ivy-covered towers and angled roofs.

The uniformed driver turned around and smiled at his passenger. "Talbot Castle, Mr. Larry."

Larry stepped out of the car. He was a tall, sturdy young man with thick brown hair. His dark eyes filled with sorrow when he saw the ancient oak trees he used to climb with his brother. Larry glanced away and saw the town and countryside below. He remembered the stories his nanny had told him and his brother of armored knights who had fought battles on the very same land. Sometimes she told them stories about mysterious monsters that roamed the woods.

Sudden storm clouds swallowed the sunshine, and dark shadows lurked around corners of the castle. Silent servants hurried to the car to take Larry's luggage. Shrugging off his gloomy thoughts, he followed them into the castle.

The long entrance hall was hung with aging tapestries and yellowed portraits of long-dead Talbots. Suits of armor stood ghostly guard beneath the cracked paintings. Their empty eyeslits gazed blankly ahead.

Larry went directly to the castle library. He knew he would find his father there. The library was a big room paneled in dark, polished wood. Shelves stuffed with leather-bound books covered the dark, paneled walls. As Larry entered the library, he heard the first pattering of rain against the tall, vine-covered windows.

The old-fashioned stuffed chairs were placed just where Larry remembered them. And the same thick, worn carpets lay before the grand fireplace just as they always had. Two men stood by the fire. The smaller one stepped forward. Larry felt a shock of tenderness and fear as he shook hands with his father, Sir John.

Larry's powerful hand completely covered his father's delicate fingers. Sir John was a short, dignified man. His gray hair was combed straight back from his high forehead. Dark, sharp eyes took in every detail of his son's appearance. Sir John smiled.

"Welcome home, Larry."

"I'm glad to be here, Father." Larry tossed his hat on a mahogany table. "Hasn't changed much, has it?"

"Not in three hundred years," Sir John said proudly. "Except for a few modern conveniences." Then he gestured to the tall, athletic man standing by the fire. "Do you remember Paul Montford?"

Colonel Montford adjusted his tweed jacket and stepped forward to shake hands with Larry. "I just dropped in to say hello. Welcome home, Larry."

As Larry shook Montford's hand, his mind filled again with memories, and he said, "We used to swipe apples together." Larry peered into the man's long, serious face, trying to find traces of the boy he once knew.

"Well, now he's Chief Constable of the district," Sir John put in with a touch of amusement.

"That reminds me," Montford said. "I've got to get to work. See you about nine, Sir John? Glad to have you back, Larry."

The policeman strode to the door.

"Thanks. Good-bye," Larry called after Montford. He joined his father before the crackling fire. "So Paul turned out to be a cop."

Sir John was amused by his son's American slang. "A cop?"

"Yeah, a cop, a policeman, you know." Larry's eyes strayed to the oil painting above the mantel; the face in the portrait was a lot like his own. Larry felt sad seeing his older brother, John Talbot, who was dressed in the black robes of a judge. Sir John and

4

THE WOLF MAN

Larry were all that remained of the great Talbot clan.

Sir John prodded the fire with a long metal poker.

Larry spoke gently. "Father, I'm sorry about John."

Sir John looked away and put aside the poker. "Your brother's death was a blow to all of us. Sit down, Larry, won't you?"

Larry perched uncomfortably on the arm of a chair. His father still talked to him as if he were a child, and Larry felt just as nervous as he had in the old days.

Sir John continued, "You know, Larry, a tradition has developed regarding the Talbot sons. The eldest usually gets all the attention. The younger son frequently resents his position and leaves home, just as you did."

"Yes, Father, but I'm *here* now," Larry said reassuringly. He was surprised to hear Sir John speak openly of their problem. But perhaps grief had made his father less reserved.

"But isn't it sad that it took a hunting accident and your brother's death to bring us together?" Sir John asked solemnly. The lord of the manor did not like to display much emotion, but his feelings toward Larry ran deep. For the first time there was a warmth in Sir John's voice that revealed his love for his younger son.

Larry moved toward his father. "You and I are not so bad. I've read every bit of news about you. I was very proud when you won the Belden Prize for Research."

Sir John, a noted astronomer and scholar, nodded modestly. "The whole business between us was probably my fault, Larry. You see, family tradition insists that we Talbots be rather formal fellows. And frequently this has been carried to very unhappy extremes."

"No kidding!" Larry agreed enthusiastically. He could hardly believe his father was saying this after all these years. Although he and his father had been distant, Larry did not hold a grudge. Now they could make up for all the lost time.

Sir John smiled and extended his hand once again. "Larry, let's decide, you and I, that there shall be no more such reserve between us."

Larry chuckled to himself. His father still sounded like a school principal delivering a speech. "I'll do everything I can, sir," Larry agreed. Father and son shook hands heartily.

"I'm glad to hear that," Sir John said. "In the eighteen years you've been away, I'm sure you have learned many things that will benefit the estate. In a great many ways we Welsh are a backward people, but don't quote me."

The great oak door of the library creaked open. The butler and a footman entered carrying a heavy wooden box.

"It's from London, sir," the footman said. "I think it's the new part for the telescope."

"Ah, yes," said Sir John, recalling the part he had ordered a few weeks before. With everything that had happened in the last few days, he had completely forgotten. "Come along to the attic, Larry. It's an observatory now."

Sir John and Larry followed the servants out of the library and up a great winding staircase. Larry's legs grew heavier and heavier as he climbed the worn stone steps. He suddenly realized how tired his travels had left him.

They soon arrived at a glassed-in room built into one of the castle's angled roofs. In the center of the room stood a raised platform. A huge brass telescope was mounted on the platform. The telescope had a heavy, solid metal base covered with wheels and dials and buttons. Sections of the glass ceiling could be rolled back so that the viewer could get a closer look at the stars.

At this moment, however, rain drummed on the glass dome as Roberts, the butler, along with the footman, applied crowbars to the creaking crate. After a few minutes they carefully pried off the lid. Larry dug into the rustling tangle of packing straw to expose the precious contents. He insisted on installing the new lenses himself. Like the eager boy he'd been when he left, Larry longed to show his father something he was good at. By the time he was finished, the rain had stopped. "There you are, sir. I think that does it," he said.

Sir John put down the book he had been reading. "I'll have a look at it." Larry watched nervously as his father took his place on the platform before the huge telescope. Sir John turned several knobs to adjust his focus through the eyepiece. He focused the powerful magnifying glass on a car driving through a quaint village street below. The telescope was so powerful, Sir John could read the car's license plate. "Hmm, excellent. Where did you learn such precision work?"

"At an optical company in California. We supplied instruments for many observatories," Larry said. He realized how little his father knew about him. Letters from home had stopped after his mother's death years ago. Larry had stopped writing soon after that.

"Are you interested in astronomy?" Sir John asked hopefully.

Larry shrugged his large shoulders. "Not especially. But I'm great with tools. In fact, I've done a lot of work with astronomical instruments. But when it comes to theory, I'm pretty much of an amateur."

Sir John continued to peer through the telescope. His fingers expertly twirled small knobs and dials, making fine adjustments. "All astronomers are amateurs," Sir John said dryly. "When it comes to the heavens, there is only one professional." At last he leaned away from the eyepiece, satisfied. "Fine. Well, I've got some things to do before lunch. I'll leave you to it." Sir John stood up briskly and left the room.

Curious about the telescope, Larry looked through it. He smiled at the view of the little Welsh village below. Then he swung the tube until something caught his eye in a window above an antique shop. A pretty young woman stood in the window admiring her reflection in a hand mirror. She seemed to pay particular attention to her sparkling earrings. Larry scanned down to the sign painted on the shop window:

CHARLES CONLIFFE
ANTIQUES
BOUGHT AND SOLD

Moving the telescope down a bit farther, he saw a clutter of antiques through the shop's window. Larry decided to visit the shop after lunch and a nap.

Later that afternoon, Larry stood smiling at his reflection in the window of the antique shop. He adjusted his tie and stepped jauntily through the door. A bell jangled as he entered.

The antique shop had a low ceiling and a creaky wooden floor. Although the sun streamed through the thick front window, most of the shop remained dark and gloomy. The shop was jammed with musty furniture, racks of old china, and odd relics of family estates that had gone to ruin.

The pretty blond girl he had admired through the telescope looked up from a showcase of ornate jewelry when he came through the door. She seemed almost too young and lively for this graveyard of old furniture. He wondered if she could be Charles Conliffe's daughter.

"Good afternoon, sir. May I help you?" Gwen Conliffe asked in a lilting Welsh accent. Here was a handsome stranger. She did not often get to meet new people, except for the occasional tourist.

"Why, yes. I'm looking for a gift. I was thinking of buying earrings," Larry said. His dark eyes flashed with amusement at the joke he was about to play.

Gwen lifted a black velvet tray from the case. "Certainly. We've some very nice earrings. These diamond ones are very smart, or how about these pearl ones?"

"No, I don't think any of those will do," Larry replied. "What I'm really looking for is something golden, perhaps half-moon shaped . . . with spangles . . ."

Gwen's blue eyes clouded with confusion. The stranger's brown eyes seemed intelligent. He had the bold manner of an American. "Oh, I'm sorry. I'm afraid we haven't anything like that just now."

"Yes, you have," Larry insisted. "Don't you remember—on your dressing table, up in your room?"

"In my room?" Gwen was very surprised, almost frightened. But there was something charming about the man, despite the hint of danger.

Larry asked, "Yes, would you mind getting them for me?"

"Well, I . . . they're not for sale," she stammered, putting down the velvet tray. "Well, perhaps my father can help you. I'll call him."

"No, that won't be necessary." Larry stopped her. He strolled over to a rack of walking sticks. The old floor groaned beneath his steps, and the rack of canes rattled like dry bones. "Since I can't have the earrings, maybe I'll buy one of these." Larry just wanted a chance to talk to the girl a little longer.

"How did you know about the earrings in my room?" Gwen asked.

"Oh, I just know. Every time I see a beautiful girl, I know everything about her, just like that." Larry snapped his fingers.

Gwen was flattered, in spite of her better judgment. "What kind of cane would you like—everyday or formal?"

"Oh, it doesn't matter," Larry said casually, examining the sticks.

Gwen lifted an expensive cane. "This one is very smart. Solid gold top."

Larry shook his head. "I don't think that will do."

She held up a cane topped with a carved Scottie dog. "Well, how about the little dog? That would suit you."

"No, thanks." Larry pulled another cane from the rack. A large silver wolf's head covered the top of its ebony shaft. Larry stared at the cane as if he were hypnotized. The wolf's head's tarnished teeth formed a terrible grin, and its ruby eyes blazed with an eerie light. Larry felt a shiver run up his arm, and the hairs on the back of his neck stirred. There was something dreadful about the cane. He felt his soul being gripped by a powerful evil.

Larry tried to shake off this eerie feeling. He turned the cane upside down and pretended to play golf. "This would make a good putter."

Gwen smiled. "I guess it would."

"I like the dog's head on top of the cane," Larry went on. He flipped the cane upright in his hand. He could not put it down.

"No, that's a wolf," Gwen corrected him. The cane had been in the shop for as long as she could remember. No one would look at the hideous thing for long, much less purchase it.

"A wolf?" Larry looked more closely at the heavily carved silver. He noticed a five-pointed star engraved at the base of the wolf's shaggy throat. "A wolf and a star. What does it mean?"

"Well, I thought you said you knew everything," Gwen teased.

"Oh, I do. But this is only wood and silver, and it doesn't have pretty blue eyes," Larry flirted.

"Well, the cane is priced at three pounds," Gwen said in her most businesslike manner.

"Three pounds? Fifteen dollars—for an old cane?"

"Well, it's a very rare piece, and it shows the wolf and the pentagram, that five-pointed star. That's the sign of the werewolf," Gwen explained. Maybe he would come to his senses and leave the cursed thing in the rack. She had often asked her father to get rid of it, but the practical shopkeeper refused.

Larry frowned. "Werewolf? What's that?" He faintly remembered a frightening story his nanny had once told him.

"A werewolf is a human being who sometimes changes into a wolf," Gwen said, as if something so outrageous were perfectly true—even ordinary.

"You mean a wolf that runs around on all fours and bites and snaps and bays at the moon?" Larry asked. How could anyone take such nonsense seriously?

"Even worse than that sometimes," Gwen said earnestly.

Larry stared into her lovely blue eyes. "'What big eyes you have, Grandma!'"

Gwen recognized the quotation from the old fairy tale. "'Little Red Riding Hood' was a werewolf story," she said, walking away. The American kept getting too close to her. She had heard they were very bold. "Of course," she said from the other side of the counter, "there have been many other werewolf stories. There's even an old poem:

> 'Even a man who is pure in heart,
> And says his prayers by night,
> May become a wolf when the wolfsbane blooms,
> And the autumn moon is bright.' "

A slow chill spread over Larry. The curious verse had such an ominous ring. The cane seemed to burn in his hand, and the ruby eyes seemed to glow with malice. This is ridiculous, he thought to himself. The dim little shop suddenly appeared even smaller and darker. Creepy shadows seemed to climb the walls. The air smelled musty as a tomb.

"What's this pentagram business?" Larry asked, trying once again to break the gloomy mood.

"Every werewolf is marked with that star. Legend has it that the werewolf always sees the symbol in the palm of his next victim." Like all the villagers, Gwen knew her legends well.

"Look, lady, if you're trying to scare me out of here, it's not working," Larry said, only half joking. Then he handed her three one-pound notes. "I'll take the cane."

Gwen laughed. She was glad to know the cane would soon be gone. She realized she had frightened the man with silly old stories, but he had frightened her with that strange business about her earrings. "Please tell me—have you ever seen me before?"

"Of course," said Larry. "How do you think I knew about the earrings?"

"Well, I can't remember ever . . ." Gwen knew she would remember such a handsome fellow. She escorted Larry to the shop door.

The door bell jangled over his head. He said, "I'll tell you what we'll do. We'll take a little walk tonight and talk it over."

"No!" Gwen cried. After all, he was a stranger.

"I'll see you at eight," Larry said, as if he hadn't heard her. They stood outside the shop in the fresh autumn air.

"No!" Gwen repeated firmly. Why did he think he could have such power over her?

They both turned at the sudden rumble of cart wheels and jingling bells. Through the arched village gate came a cart pulled by a tired horse in a colorful harness. An old Gypsy woman held the reins in her withered hands. She wore a bright kerchief tied over wispy white hair. Her sour face frowned above a black blouse and a necklace of gold coins. A flowing embroidered skirt fell almost to the ground, dangerously close to the turning cart wheels.

A larger wagon followed close behind the small cart. The wagon swayed on wobbling wheels. Silver bells swung from the wagon's curved roof. Gwen knew Gypsies believed that silver drove away demons and evil spirits.

The driver was a dark man with a thick black mustache. A vest covered his embroidered white shirt. He held the reins to a sleek black horse. He scowled at the villagers, his dark eyes smoldering under what seemed like a single thick eyebrow.

"Gypsies, huh?" Larry asked.

Gwen nodded. "Yes, they're fortune-tellers. They pass through here each autumn."

"You know, I haven't had my fortune told in years. Let's go tonight?" Larry asked, still hoping to get a date.

"No!" Gwen closed the shop door behind her with a loud jangle of the bell.

"Fine. I'll be here at eight," Larry called through the glass.

Chapter 2
Murder in the Marsh

The wind howled around Talbot Castle. The sun had long since set behind the jagged hills, and a full moon had risen brightly overhead.

Dinner was a formal ordeal, with old silverware laboriously polished for the occasion. The long table, supported by carved animal-claw legs, was covered by a crisply ironed tablecloth and weighted down with heavy old, silver candlesticks. Larry felt as if he were eating in a funeral parlor.

After dinner, Larry and his father went into the library. The conversation turned to Larry's newly purchased wolf's-head cane. Sir John's curiosity was aroused by the unusual symbol underneath the wolf's head.

"Yes, this symbol is the sign of the werewolf," Sir John said while he examined the cane.

"It's just a legend, isn't it?" Larry asked.

"Yes, but like most legends, it probably has some basis in fact.

16

Perhaps it's an ancient explanation of the dual personality in each of us. How does it go?" Sir John recited:

> " 'Even a man who is pure in heart,
> And says his prayers by night,
> May become a wolf when the wolfsbane blooms,
> And the autumn moon is bright.' "

Larry jumped up from his chair, the cane seeming to pull him from his seat. "That's funny. That's the same poem the girl in the antique shop mentioned."

"Oh, you've met Gwen Conliffe, have you?" his father asked.

"So that's her name. I met her while I was looking around the town," Larry said casually.

Sir John smiled. "Naturally. Continue to look the town over. I want you to know not only the pretty girls, but the old men and women, and the young men. Get to know all about them, Larry. They're nice people. They're your people. After all, you're going to run the estate." Once Larry inherited Talbot Castle, he would be the master of the village, as the Talbots had been for centuries.

With his brother gone, Larry's fate was mapped out. He tried to feel happy about it, and not like an animal caught in a trap. "Of course, I want to know all of them," he replied dutifully.

"You seem to have made a pretty good start," Sir John said. "Run along. Get on with the good work."

"All right. Thanks. Good night." Larry strode toward the large oak doors.

"Good night," his father called, already lost in another of his beloved books.

Gwen stepped out of the antique shop into the foggy street. Above the rooftops, a big harvest moon passed in and out of the clouds like a great, grinning skull. She pulled the door shut with a jangling of the shop bell. The village clock chimed eight times. Gwen nearly jumped out of her skin as someone suddenly stepped from a nearby doorway. Then she saw the person's handsome face.

"Oh!" Gwen cried. "It's you!"

"Whom did you expect?" Larry asked.

"Nobody. I told you I couldn't go out with you," Gwen replied. A tiny smile tugged at the edges of her pretty mouth.

"But you wore those earrings I like," Larry observed.

"Well, that was just because I . . ." Gwen was glad it was too dark for Larry to see her blush. She had harbored a small hope that the handsome stranger would indeed return.

"Aw, come on. I don't want to go alone. I'm really afraid of the dark. And you see, I brought my cane." Larry held up the silver-topped cane. Moonlight glistened on the silver fangs.

Gwen called, "Jenny!"

A dark-haired young woman, not nearly as pretty as Gwen, came out of the antique shop.

"This is Jenny Williams," Gwen informed Larry. "She wants to have her fortune told, too." Gwen had reasoned that bringing a friend along might slow the American down. He was handsome, but so pushy!

18

Jenny smiled. "I'm very pleased to meet you, Mr. . . . um . . ."

"Ah . . . just call me Larry."

"If you don't mind . . . Larry," Jenny agreed.

"Well . . ." Larry was disappointed that he and Gwen would not be alone, but what could he do? Two pretty girls were better than none. Jenny and Gwen hooked their arms through Larry's, and the three went off in a jolly mood.

Before long, their feet crunched through drifts of dry leaves in the dark woods where the Gypsies camped. Wind whistled through bare branches. The air was heavy with the sweet, decaying smell of autumn. A mist coming from the soggy marsh swirled around their knees.

The new friends stopped near a shrub glowing with white blossoms, bright in the moonlight.

"Oh, look!" Jenny cried, stooping to inhale the flowers' haunting fragrance.

"Wolfsbane," Gwen said.

" 'Even a man who is pure in heart . . .' " Jenny recited the poem as she picked the snowy blooms. Larry and Gwen chuckled while Jenny completed the familiar rhyme. " '. . . And says his prayers by night/ May become a wolf when the wolfsbane blooms/ And the autumn moon is bright.' "

"So you know the poem, too?" Larry asked as they continued walking through the misty woods. The cane began to feel heavy in his hands.

"Of course. Everyone knows about werewolves," Jenny replied. Everyone who grew up in Wales knew all sorts of wonderful and strange legends about heroes, little people, ghosts, and, of course, men who change into wolves.

Soon Larry, Gwen, and Jenny smelled smoke. They saw a campfire crackling between the painted Gypsy wagons. A horse as black as midnight stood nearby, tied to a tree. The moon lit up the branches of the trees, making them look like the arms and fingers of skeletons; they almost seemed to reach right inside the Gypsies' tents.

The three friends recognized the Gypsy known as Bela. His dark face was barely visible in the flickering firelight, except for the thick black lines that formed his mustache and eyebrow. His gold hoop earrings gleamed as he stared at the rising moon.

Jenny felt a tingly thrill of fear and clutched the flowers to her chest. Then she boldly stepped forward and said, "We've come to have our fortunes told. Can you really read the future?"

Bela's dark eyes locked on the girl. "I will not disappoint you, my lady. Will you come inside, please?"

The Gypsy stepped back to allow Jenny to enter the tent.

"Do you mind if I go first?" the girl asked her friends.

"No, go right ahead," Larry said.

"Go on, silly," Gwen urged.

Inside the tent Jenny sat across a round table from Bela. A tin lantern dangled from the center pole. Animal skulls hung in a gruesome cluster beneath the lantern. Weird shadows played across Bela's sullen face. His dark eyes never left Jenny's, even as the girl nervously looked around the tent and fiddled with her wolfsbane bouquet.

THE WOLF MAN

A crystal ball sparkled in the middle of a shabby velvet table-cloth. The air smelled of paprika and other exotic spices, masking the musky odor of some kind of animal.

The Gypsy handed Jenny a worn deck of tarot cards. She noted with a little shock that his ring finger was longer than the others and that his palms were hairy. She glanced up and found his black eyes still fixed on her. Bela's deep voice growled, "Cut them."

Jenny lifted off part of the long, curiously painted deck.

While Larry and Gwen waited outside, the old Gypsy woman stepped from another tent and into the campfire's glow. White hair straggled from beneath her colorful kerchief. Thick hoop earrings and a necklace of gold coins caught the dancing light.

Her name was Maleva. She glared at the strangers. She was sick of tourists, who thought her deepest beliefs were only quaint parlor games. If they only knew!

Larry saw the old woman's sulky stare. Feeling uncomfortable and seeing his chance to be alone with Gwen, he said, "We didn't come down to listen in on Jenny, did we?"

"No," Gwen agreed.

"Maybe if you took a little walk with me, I could tell your fortune," Larry teased.

They walked a short way through the forest, then stopped beneath a tree whose crooked branches hung above their heads.

"So you're a fortune-teller?" Gwen challenged.

Larry smiled. "Uh-huh."

"Is that how you knew about the earrings?" The mystery still

21

puzzled her.

"Not exactly," Larry said. "You see, a telescope has a sharp eye. It brings the stars so close, you feel you can almost touch them."

"A telescope?" Gwen asked. Now she was really confused.

"Sure. And it does the same thing to people in their rooms. That is, if you point it in the right direction," Larry replied.

Gwen was indignant. "You wouldn't!"

"I wanted to test the telescope. So I focused on the village, and all of a sudden there you were," Larry explained.

"From now on I'll be sure to draw the curtains," Gwen said sharply.

"Oh, don't do that. I mean, not because of me. I . . . I mean, well, you know what I mean," Larry stammered.

"Yes, I'm afraid I do," Gwen said. "But it's only fair to tell you I'm engaged to be married very soon. In fact, I really shouldn't be here."

"But you are here," replied Larry.

Back in the Gypsy tent, Jenny twirled the wolfsbane and eagerly asked, "Can you tell me when I'm going to be married?"

Bela looked up from the spread of tarot cards. A strange light glittered in the murky depths of his eyes. One card showed Death, a skeleton wielding a rusty scythe. On another card, jagged lightning struck a tower with flames leaping from its upper windows. The moon appeared on the next card, and the evil features of an angry wolf were pictured on the one that followed.

Bela pulled at his lower lip, exposing long yellow teeth.

Suddenly he snatched Jenny's wolfsbane in his fist and tossed the white flowers on the floor. Then he stared moodily into space.

Jenny looked at him with fear nipping at her heart. Bela leaned his head on his hand, brushing dark hair from his forehead. The hair had covered the dark outline of a five-pointed star across the Gypsy's brow.

"What did you see?" Jenny was worried. Why wouldn't the Gypsy speak? Had he seen some horrible fate in the cards? The man looked so terribly sad.

Bela straightened in his chair, remembering his purpose. His peculiar hands stretched across the table.

"Your hands, please," he said. "Your left hand shows your past. Your right hand shows your future."

Bela took Jenny's hands, palms up, in his. The Gypsy's hands felt hot and hairy. He looked down and saw the mark of the pentagram on the girl's right palm. Then it faded. Bela's face was grim. His black eyes slowly rose to meet her frightened gaze.

Jenny snatched her hand back. "What's the matter?" she demanded.

Bela looked away from her and rose from his chair. "I can't tell you anything tonight. Come back tomorrow." Then he stepped outside the tent.

"What did you see?" Jenny persisted. "Something evil?" She felt frightened and wished she'd never come.

Bela quivered with strange emotions. "No, no. Now go away! Go quickly!" the Gypsy urged.

"Yes! I'm going!" said Jenny. She wanted more than anything

to be safe at home. She ran past Bela and into the night.

The man watched her go with an anguished expression on his dark face. He trampled the wolfsbane twigs at his feet. How he hated those white flowers! Then he covered his face with his hands.

Inside her tent old Maleva watched smoke curl from a caldron of herbs simmering on the table. She looked up as her son, Bela, entered. How he suffered! But there was nothing she could do to change his fate.

Near the wagon the black horse pawed the ground nervously. The stallion's flanks shone in the moonlight. He bucked and strained at his reins, whinnying with fear.

Jenny had gone farther into the woods, searching for Gwen and Larry, when she heard a wolf's howl pierce the night. She could hear the frightened horses snorting as they reared up on their hind legs. Jenny changed direction and now headed back to town, frantically looking for her friends.

Not far away, Larry also heard the wolf's howl. "What was that?" he asked.

"I don't know. I never heard anything like it before," Gwen replied. The sound sent shivers up her spine.

Then they heard a scream! The shriek of terror rose to a harrowing pitch. Then there was silence.

"Wait here," Larry told Gwen. He ran through the trees toward the direction of the terrible sound.

Gwen looked around the foggy, deserted woods. Being alone was even worse than facing whatever had caused that dreadful scream. "Wait! Larry!" she called after him. But he was already several yards away. Gwen's heart hammered in her chest.

Larry ran, batting back twigs with his heavy cane. Soft growls drew him to the base of a tree where something thrashed in the leaves.

Larry stopped in shock. A huge black wolf was gnawing ravenously on Jenny's limp form. He heard her give out one last breath as life left her body. Larry came to his senses and rushed toward the wolf. He had to do something! He had to save Jenny! Larry grabbed the wolf's snout and struggled to pull the snarling animal off the girl. Larry fought the wolf with all his might. They tumbled, rolling over the gnarled tree roots and broken branches.

Giant jaws gaped inches from Larry's face. Hot breath reeking of blood blasted his nostrils. Savage teeth snapped at him. As the wolf's muscular body twisted in Larry's arms, a piercing pain shot through his chest, followed by the warm trickle of blood.

New strength surged through Larry. It was a strength born of desperate fear. He had never let go of the cane, and now it seemed to come to life on its own. Larry slammed down the heavy silver wolf's head again and again on the furry beast. He heard the horrible sound of crunching bone. The wolf's dripping jaws released him, and Larry staggered to his feet, clutching his wounded chest. He hit the wolf again and again.

Finally, the wolf fell dead. Larry stumbled away and passed out on the cold, hard ground.

CHAPTER 3
The Sign of the Werewolf

Gwen ran through the foggy woods calling Larry's name.

A dark shape moved in the moonlit mist, and Gwen found Larry on the ground, writhing in agony. She did not know that the body of her friend Jenny was close by. Gwen knelt beside Larry. "What happened? What's the matter?"

Larry gasped hoarsely, "A wolf."

Just then the old Gypsy woman, Maleva, drove up in her creaking cart. Its hanging lantern cast a dim, bouncing glow.

"Help!" Gwen cried. "Please, hurry."

Maleva climbed slowly off the cart. Her old bones creaked like the worn cart wheels. Her ancient eyes took in everything, including things Gwen did not see. Maleva shuffled toward the tree. "What happened?"

"A wolf bit him," Gwen explained breathlessly.

The Gypsy woman looked down at Larry and then at the body beneath the twisted tree.

Gwen suddenly recognized the body of her friend Jenny. She screamed in horror. "Do something. Can't you help them?" she pleaded. Jenny was dead and Larry was bleeding, and this old woman was standing around as if nothing had happened.

Maleva stooped to help Gwen lift Larry onto the cart.

"You must take him home," she told the frightened girl.

Back at Talbot Castle, Sir John and Colonel Montford chatted before a cozy fire in the library.

"Big boy, isn't he?" Sir John asked. He was still amazed that his younger son now towered over him. To the small and bookish Sir John, his son's size seemed almost dangerous—but no matter how old or big he became, Larry would always be his "boy."

"Larry is huge," Montford agreed between puffs on his pipe.

"Like the red Talbots, there." Sir John pointed to the wall and a faded portrait of a hulking Welsh warrior.

"Larry should join the Guards," Montford suggested.

"Oh, no, I need him here, looking after the estate. He's had a lot of experience in America." Sir John chuckled. He was glad to have Larry home. The Talbots would continue: Larry already had his eye out for a wife.

Both men looked up as the footman opened the door for Gwen, Larry, and Maleva. Sir John and Montford rushed toward them. One glance and they knew something was terribly wrong.

Montford said, "Here, here, what's the matter?"

Larry staggered into the room. His torn clothes were spattered with clots of blood. One stain had spread like a bat's wings on his shredded shirt. Gwen struggled to support him, while Maleva hung back in the doorway.

"He was bitten by a wolf," Gwen explained.

Montford cried in surprise, "A wolf!" He'd never heard of one attacking a person. Normally, wolves were shy creatures that avoided humans.

"Nonsense, there haven't been wolves around here for years," Sir John said. Most of the wolves in Britain had died out four centuries ago, when the great medieval forests had been cleared. A few had lingered as late as 1870 in the wildernesses of Wales and Scotland. But no one had seen a living wolf in decades.

While the men puzzled, Maleva faded into the shadows.

"Where did all this happen?" Montford asked. His policeman's mind groped for facts.

Gwen answered, "In the woods, by the marsh. That woman came to help." But when Gwen turned, she found that Maleva was gone. "Where is she?"

"Who?" said Sir John.

"The Gypsy woman who helped me get Larry here," Gwen answered.

"Yes, of course," Montford agreed. He had noticed her, but his sharp eyes now caught no trace of Maleva in the hall.

Larry leaned over the table, his handsome face tortured with pain. Sir John and Gwen hovered over him, concerned.

"Jenny! Someone get Jenny!" was Larry's anguished cry.

Just then a villager rushed into the room. "Sir John! Colonel . . ." The man stopped for a moment, silenced by the

28

elegance of the library. His voice shook with excitement as he continued. "By the marsh . . ."

"Yes, yes, the marsh," Montford snapped.

"Speak up, man," Sir John urged.

Clutching his coarse cap, the villager spoke breathlessly. "Jenny. Jenny Williams . . ."

"What about her?" Sir John asked impatiently.

"She's been murdered, sir." Then the villager glanced down at his mud-caked shoes.

Sir John and Montford were shocked. They bent their heads together and talked in hushed tones. "Wolves, Gypsy woman, murder—what is this?" Sir John muttered.

"What makes you say she was murdered?" Montford demanded.

Twisting the cap nervously in his rough hands, the villager said, "Her throat, sir."

Montford snatched his hat from the table and rushed to the door. He ushered the frightened villager out of the room with him. "Come, come, let's look into this. Show me where it happened. I'll send Dr. Lloyd, Sir John," Montford called over his shoulder.

"Fine. Roberts, give me a hand with Master Larry," Sir John told the butler. "Come on, Larry," he said, putting his son's arm around his shoulder. Together, the two elderly men lifted the large, wounded man. Gwen walked behind them, afraid for Larry and wondering how a night of fun had become a night of horror.

In the woods a cluster of men surrounded the twisted tree.

Some held lanterns, but the feeble light did little to dispel the gloom. Other men clutched the leashes of nervous dogs. Whining and yipping, a terrier circled the knees of the Talbots' gamekeeper, Frank Andrews. The tall, handsome young man was Gwen's fiancé. His short light brown hair was combed to one side, and he had pleasant clear green eyes. Frank had already identified the tracks near Jenny's cold corpse as those of a large wolf.

Dr. Lloyd, the village physician, knelt beside Jenny's body. The doctor was a tall, slender man in a tasteful dark suit. His gray hair was slicked back from his high forehead. His small round eyeglasses glittered in the lantern light.

Colonel Montford was also examining the body. He called to his assistant, Mr. Twiddle, a short, chubby man in a dark suit.

"Yes, sir," Twiddle replied, coming closer to the scene. His black bowler hat was as round as he was. His dark mustache drooped like a sleeping caterpillar over his mouth.

"Take notes, Twiddle," Montford said.

Twiddle flipped open his small notebook and licked his stubby pencil. "Very good, sir."

"Jenny Williams was attacked by some large animal. Is that right, Dr. Lloyd?" Montford asked.

The doctor nodded grimly. His trained eyes surveyed the girl's mutilated body. Judging by the jagged red wound that tore her throat, the doctor instantly knew what had killed the poor girl. "The jugular vein in her throat was cut by the bite of powerful teeth. The poor girl bled to death."

Montford looked up to make sure his assistant had taken down the doctor's statement. Poor Twiddle stood frozen, his round face a mask of horror. Twiddle had never been on such a case before. Murder was rare in the peaceful little village.

"What's the matter with you, Twiddle?" Montford asked.

"I'm a little squeamish, sir," Twiddle replied in a shaking voice. He would not look in the direction of the crumpled body.

"Just write down what I told you," Montford said firmly.

"Very well, sir," Twiddle said doubtfully. He forced his eyes back down to the notebook held in his trembling hands.

Meanwhile Frank Andrews wandered away from the tree, past the other men, hoping to find clues. He searched the ground for more tracks and small twigs and bits of fur. What he found was another dead body!

Frank stooped over the corpse sprawled among the leaves. Blood gleamed like pools of black oil in the moonlight. Frank cried, "Colonel Montford! Here, sir. It's the Gypsy who passed through town this afternoon."

The investigators slogged through the fog and leaves. Dr. Lloyd took a lantern from Montford to examine Bela's body. Twiddle lagged behind.

"Was he killed by the same animal, Dr. Lloyd?" Montford asked.

"No. His skull was crushed by a heavy blow from a sharp instrument," Dr. Lloyd concluded.

"Take a note, Twiddle," Montford said.

Twiddle's voice was faint. "Very well, sir." He felt queasy and wished he'd never had that snack after supper.

Montford continued in his cool tones. "Bela the Gypsy was found dead near the body of Jenny Williams. Cause of death was a heavy blow inflicted by a sharp instrument."

The doctor observed, "His feet are bare."

"So they are, and he's fully dressed otherwise. Make a note of that, Twiddle," Montford said.

"Very well, sir,"

Frank's keen eyes saw something gleaming under the crackly leaves. "What's this?" He picked up Larry's silver-topped cane, clotted with blood.

"It's a stick with a horse's-head handle," Twiddle said, glad to finally know something.

Montford took the cane and studied the sticky handle. "That's no horse's head. That's a wolf's head."

Twiddle gasped, "Oh, Mr. Frank, them tracks back there—they belonged to a wolf!" Twiddle knew the local legends as well as any man there. He had felt sick before, but now the cold hand of superstition chilled his spine.

"Take a note, Twiddle," Montford said calmly. "A silver-handled cane mounted with wolf's head was found on scene."

"Very well, sir." Twiddle's pencil quivered over the page.

Frank rose, along with Montford. The colonel said, "Let's have a look at those tracks. Twiddle, you stay here with the bodies."

Twiddle stood over the Gypsy's corpse, nervously removing his hat to mop his brow with a polka-dot handkerchief. Twiddle sighed. He wondered which was worse—staying with the bodies, or going with the others into the mist-shrouded woods to face the unknown?

CHAPTER 4
The Disappearing Wound

As the sun rose the next morning, Larry tossed and turned in his bed. He was in the clutches of a horrible dream. He was running through the woods near his home, the howling of a wolf ringing in his ears. Suddenly he was fighting a big black beast. They rolled through a suffocating carpet of leaves. Fierce fangs foamed and snapped, tearing at the flesh beneath his throat. Pain ripped through him. Larry raised his cane and pounded the wolf's skull over and over. But in the midst of his agony he saw that the wolf had human eyes and hands!

A soft tap sounded over and over on Larry's bedroom door. His eyes snapped open. The woods vanished. He was in his own room in Talbot Castle. The monstrous vision was only a dream, and no doubt good old Roberts was bringing him coffee in bed.

Larry got out of bed. He put on a robe to ward off the damp chill of the bedroom. The door opened, and his father, Dr. Lloyd, and Colonel Montford walked in. Larry blinked at them in confusion. His heart sank as the memory of the previous night flooded his mind. He *had* been in the woods last night. Something terrible *had* happened; a picture of Jenny and the wolf flashed before his eyes.

Sir John asked, "Larry, shouldn't you be in bed?"

"I'm all right," Larry said groggily.

Montford nodded. "Good morning, Larry."

Sir John introduced the tall, serious doctor.

"You frightened us last night," Dr. Lloyd said gently. He looked at young Talbot with a professional eye.

"I'm sorry. I guess I did kind of pass out." Larry sat back down on the bed, looking up at his visitors.

Montford held the wolf's-head cane. "Is this your cane?"

"Of course," Larry said. "That's the one I killed the wolf with."

Sir John spoke carefully. "Bela the Gypsy was killed last night and your cane was found next to the body."

Larry was puzzled. "You mean Bela, the fortune-teller?"

Sir John nodded gravely.

"I only saw a wolf. He bit me. Look here." Larry stood and opened the collar of his robe. Dr. Lloyd examined the young man's bare, unmarked chest.

"That's funny," Larry said, frowning in confusion. "The wound must have healed." But how could such a deep wound heal overnight?!

Sir John said, "Colonel Montford wants to ask you some questions."

Larry was still thinking about the healed wound. "Sure, sure, go ahead," he agreed absently. He looked out the narrow window. The sun was glowing weakly through a thick shroud of clouds.

"No, I think we ought to leave him alone," Dr. Lloyd suggested. Larry was obviously in shock. He had faced a terrible ordeal in the woods last night.

"What's the matter with you, Doctor?" Sir John said. "Paul Montford wants to ask Larry some questions. Go ahead, Paul."

"Sure, ask away, but don't try to make me believe I killed a man when I know I killed a wolf," Larry said, an edge of hysteria creeping into his voice. What was wrong with them? He knew what had happened in the woods last night. They could ask Gwen. Was he still dreaming?

The doctor patted Larry's shoulder and spoke as if to a child. "Yes, yes, we're all a little bit confused." Dr. Lloyd drew Montford aside and said quietly, "He needs a good rest."

Montford listened to the doctor's opinion and considered Larry's dazed behavior. He left the cane on a table and said, "We'll talk to you later, Larry. Come on, Doctor."

Dr. Lloyd asked, "Coming, Sir John?"

Sir John replied, "Yes, I'll be down in a minute." The door clicked shut. "Now, Larry, will you stop worrying and let me handle this?"

Larry went to the table and lifted the cane. He stared into those cold ruby eyes and frowned. His voice was a harsh growl. "Yeah, but they're treating me like I'm crazy."

A few minutes later in the castle library, Colonel Montford perched on the arm of a leather chair. Dr. Lloyd stood nearby, while

Sir John paced before the tall, vine-covered windows.

The colonel said, "I don't accuse Larry of foul play, Sir John, but after all, two people are dead and I am Chief Constable."

"That's no reason to make a great mystery out of it," Dr. Lloyd countered. "You talk like a detective in a novel."

"Then, what about this nonexistent wolf?" Montford persisted. *Something* had torn out Jenny Williams's throat.

"Please, gentlemen," Sir John said reasonably. "There must be a simple explanation." He lived in a tidy, scholarly world where the answers to everything could be found in the pages of books. He was sure all mysteries could be solved by modern science. So Sir John offered what he considered a likely explanation for last night's events. "A dog or a wolf attacked Jenny Williams. That's proven. When she cried for help, Larry and Bela came to her rescue. It was dark. In the excitement and confusion the Gypsy was killed."

Colonel Montford rose and crossed the room to join Sir John. "What about Bela's bare feet?" the policeman asked.

The doctor suggested, "Well, he just didn't have time to put on his shoes."

Colonel Montford remained suspicious. "Larry insists he received a wound." He turned to the doctor. "Surely a wound can't heal overnight."

"Larry imagined he had been bitten. After all, the beast jumped at him and tore his coat to shreds," Sir John explained.

Dr. Lloyd observed, "Right now, the patient is mentally disturbed. Shock can cause confusion. I'd rather you didn't bother him with questions for a while."

Sir John agreed. "You policemen are always in such a hurry—as if dead men hadn't all eternity to wait."

Montford joked, "Well, you'll be declaring me a mental case next."

The doctor smiled. "Oh, no, I wouldn't dare."

Montford said, "Thank you. In return, I won't question your patient until you think best."

CHAPTER 5
The Tomb

Larry couldn't rest. Why didn't anyone believe him? Where was the wolf bite? How could they think he would confuse a man with the fur and fangs of a wild beast?

He paced his room until he felt its walls were closing in on him. He needed fresh air and trees, and nothing but the sky over his head.

Larry got dressed and went for a walk to clear his mind. He wandered through swirling mist and soon found himself before the quaint village church, looming like a lost ship in the clammy fog.

Two ladies walked down the church's wide stone steps. Nearby a horse's hooves clopped on the cobblestones. The horse was pulling an open black wagon bearing a plain pine coffin. The women watched the wagon roll slowly by.

"It's the Gypsy fortune-teller," one of the women said.

The other woman pointed at Larry. "Look! There is the man

who killed him."

Larry shuddered and then felt a flash of anger. Why was everyone accusing him of Bela's murder? He had killed a wolf. No amount of fog or fear could cloud the facts. He had smelled the blood on its breath, felt the snapping jaws reach for his throat. And yet, where was the wound? If only Gwen had found him a little sooner; she would be able to tell them all the truth.

Like a sleepwalker compelled by some dark spell, Larry followed the rumbling wagon around the church to the graveyard. Crooked, weathered tombstones poked up through a dense layer of fog. Weary gravediggers carried Bela's cheap coffin through a rusty iron gate.

Larry waited until the gravediggers had carried the coffin into a large stone crypt. He quietly followed them inside. The tomb reeked of dust and decay. A handful of candles flickered feebly in the gloom. Jumbled bones lay about. Spiders crawled over dried bouquets of long-dead flowers; their cobwebs hung like lace curtains from deep stone arches and carved columns. Larry quickly hid behind a thick pillar to watch what would happen.

The gravediggers lifted the heavy coffin onto a platform in the center of the stone chamber. Then they hurried away. Larry removed his hat and walked slowly toward the unpainted coffin. He had to know the truth! He overcame his fear and raised the rough, creaking lid. He glanced inside at the mangled remains of the unfortunate Gypsy. Then Larry dropped the splintery lid and turned to run. But when he heard voices, he slipped back into the shadows of the tomb.

"But, my dear woman, we can't bury this man without prayer," said a balding, pudgy minister. He wore a neat black suit and white clerical collar. Maleva shuffled at his side, her old back bent with grief and the weight of many years.

"There's nothing to pray for, sir," the old Gypsy said in her slow, toneless voice. "Bela has entered a much better world than this—at least so you ministers always say, sir."

"And so it is, but that's no reason to hold a pagan celebration," the minister chided. "I hear your people are coming to town tonight for dancing, and singing, and making merry."

Maleva's dark eyes flashed in her weathered face. "For a thousand years we Gypsies have buried our dead this way. I couldn't break the custom even if I wanted to."

"Fighting against superstition is as hard as fighting against Satan himself," the minister said sadly. He had decided that he could no more sway this stubborn woman than change the cycle of the moon. The minister left the tomb, praying for the souls of the old woman and her dead son.

With the minister gone, the silence of death once again reigned in the cool darkness. Larry watched Maleva lift the coffin's creaking lid. His face twisted with anguish as Maleva spoke in her sad, monotonous voice:

"'The way you walked was thorny, through no fault of your own. But as the rain enters the soil, the river enters the sea, so tears run to a predestined end. Your suffering is over, Bela, my son. Now you will find peace.'" Maleva bowed her kerchiefed head. She closed the coffin and shuffled out of the tomb.

Larry ran to the coffin. He fell across the wooden box and sobbed. Had he really killed Maleva's son? Had he only imagined the wolf? Was he losing his mind?

CHAPTER 6
The Visitors

The antique dealer, Charles Conliffe, sat in the cozy parlor behind his shop. His daughter, Gwen, stood nervously looking out the window. She had made herself a cup of tea, but it now sat neglected on a small carved table. Gwen stared at the village as if she had never seen it before. She felt that her world had changed overnight into a strange, horrible place where anything might happen.

Gwen's father watched her with concern. He was a short man with thinning gray hair and old-fashioned eyeglasses. He wore a bow tie and conservative gray suit. Most of his days were spent in the cluttered antique shop, among the old things he treasured. Since his wife's death, Gwen had been his only companion.

Mr. Conliffe tried to comfort his daughter. "But, my dear, you've done nothing wrong. Why don't you go to your room and lie down?"

"I don't want to be alone, Father. When I close my eyes, I see

Jenny. I'd rather stay out here," said Gwen. Her blue eyes were clouded with visions of her friend's mangled corpse.

"Why, of course, my dear, of course," Mr. Conliffe said gently. He heard the shop bell jangle and put down his cup of tea. When he stepped into the shop adjoining the parlor, he saw four women, including Jenny's mother, Mrs. Williams. "Well, ladies, what can I do for you?" he asked courteously.

Mrs. Williams wore black mourning clothes. Her red-rimmed eyes gleamed with hysteria. "Where is she?" she snapped.

In the next room, Gwen listened tensely.

"Why, what do you want to know?" the antique dealer asked mildly.

"I want to know why she left my little Jenny all alone with that Gypsy!" Mrs. Williams's voice rose to a desperate shriek.

"I suppose she didn't want to be there while Jenny's fortune was being told." Mr. Conliffe answered, recalling what Gwen had told him.

"What a lie!" Mrs. Williams shrilled. "You know she just wanted to walk off in the dark with—"

"You mustn't speak of my Gwen like that," Mr. Conliffe interrupted. He felt great sympathy for Jenny's mother, but he would not tolerate anyone speaking ill of his dear Gwen.

"Listen to him," Mrs. Williams said to her companions. "There's a fine father for you."

"How dare you permit her to go out with other men when she's engaged to Frank Andrews!" the incredibly plump Mrs. Wykes accused.

In the parlor Gwen felt a stab of anguish. If only she hadn't walked away! More than anything in the world she wished she had stayed home last night.

"She didn't do anything wrong," Mr. Conliffe defended his daughter. He knew that in her grief Mrs. Williams was just trying to find someone to blame for the tragedy.

"Anything wrong!" Mrs. Williams sneered. "It was because of her that my little Jenny was killed." She burst into tears.

"Now that's enough!" Gwen's father exclaimed. This was outrageous. Some kind of animal had killed Jenny. It wasn't Gwen's fault. She was in enough pain already without having her friend's mother make accusations.

At that moment Larry Talbot peered through the shop's glass door.

"She's to blame," Mrs. Williams persisted. "I always knew that innocent face was just a—"

"Come on, now, outside, outside all of you," Mr. Conliffe said soothingly. He couldn't bear the idea of Gwen's hearing these cruel lies. He ushered the women to the door.

Mrs. Williams threatened him. "You'll not get rid of me before I know the truth." She thrust her face close to Mr. Conliffe's. "I want to know what she was doing while my little Jenny was being murdered!"

Just then the door swung open. The brass bell jangled loudly as Larry ducked through the low door. Mrs. Williams continued to rant and rave. "I'll tell you what she was doing."

"All right, tell me," Larry challenged.

THE WOLF MAN

The women turned to stare at him with eyes full of hate. "Come on, come on, speak up," Larry growled, stepping toward them. A gleam in his eye promised violence; his fingers clutched the cruel cane.

"Don't you dare touch me," Mrs. Williams said. She backed away in horror as Larry towered over her. The other women gingerly brushed past his angry bulk to slip out the door.

Mrs. Williams called over her shoulder to Mr. Conliffe, "You and your fine daughter have not heard the last of this!'

Larry glared after the women. He was furious. He clenched his huge fists. How dare they accuse Gwen! How dare they judge what they did not understand! Taking a deep breath, he struggled to control his raging temper. His voice sounded calmer than he felt. "What's gotten into them?" he asked Mr. Conliffe.

"I really don't know," the older man said, spreading his hands upward.

Larry fidgeted with his hat. Rage was replaced with regret. "I'm sorry about getting Gwen into this mess. We just went for a walk," he said.

"I trust my daughter, sir," Mr. Conliffe replied stiffly. He knew that young Talbot had grown up in Wales. He also knew that one day Larry would be the lord of the manor, but he still didn't like his pushy ways.

Larry fretted. "I hope Gwen didn't hear all that. Is she in?"

"Yes, she's in the parlor," Mr. Conliffe reported.

"May I see her, please?" Larry asked.

His voice was so gentle and concerned that Gwen's father

softened. "Why, of course," he agreed.

Larry nodded. "Thank you."

Mr. Conliffe left the young people alone and went into the shop to work on the accounts.

Gwen was surprised to see Larry. She dabbed at her tears with a lace handkerchief.

Larry looked from the small parlor to the cramped shop, knowing Gwen must have heard Mrs. Williams's shrill accusations. "Oh, you . . . heard them?"

Gwen nodded sadly and walked to the fireplace. Her blond head drooped. "Yes. I suppose you can't blame them too much. It's kind of a mess, isn't it?"

"I came over here to tell you how sorry I am about Jenny," Larry said quietly. He could barely breathe in the crowded little room, cluttered with frayed, lace-draped furniture and fragile knickknacks.

Gwen struggled to hold back her tears. "Tell me, just exactly what did happen?"

"Well, I . . . I saw a wolf attacking her and I killed it. In the fight it bit me, but this morning there was no sign of the wound. Now they're trying to make me believe I killed Bela, the fortune-teller," Larry said. But even as he spoke, he was troubled by all the contradictions. He knew what he'd seen, but who would believe him?

"Maybe there wasn't a wolf," Gwen suggested. "It was dark and foggy and, well . . . perhaps the story I told you about the werewolf confused you."

Larry felt another surge of rage. Didn't she remember that eerie howl? "Why does everyone insist I'm confused?" he asked angrily.

The shop bell jangled again. Gwen's father looked up from his account books and saw Frank Andrews leading his black-and-tan Welsh terrier on a leash. The curly-haired dog sniffed interestedly at the carved paws of the table legs.

The antique dealer patted the terrier and smiled at his daughter's fiancé. "Hello, Frank."

"Hello, Mr. Conliffe. Is Gwen in?" Frank asked pleasantly.

Mr. Conliffe hesitated. "Yes, but . . . she has a visitor."

Frank guessed, "Larry Talbot?"

"Yes," Mr. Conliffe confirmed.

"Well, that's all right," Frank said without jealousy. "I want to see him, too." The athletic young man walked quickly to the parlor. The terrier's claws clicked across the wooden floor.

Gwen leaned on the mantel. She felt confused and a bit embarrassed when her fiancé appeared in the room. "L-Larry, this is Frank Andrews."

Larry extended his hand. Frank's dog suddenly bristled and burst into a fit of wild barking. Larry wanted to cover his ears to block out the noise. His eyes fixed on the creature's flashing white teeth. He longed to run, but the walls seemed to close in around him, and all possible escape was blocked by the parlor furniture.

Frank was shocked. Welshies were a nervous breed, but his dog was usually so friendly. He pulled back on the leash. "Quiet!" he commanded, but the dog did not respond. Frank had rarely heard the terrier bark so fiercely, even during the hunt.

"You'd better take him outside, Frank," Gwen said.

"All right. Come on, come on." Frank dragged the maddened terrier out of the shop. The dog scrabbled and barked all the way to the door.

Larry was glad to see the nasty beast go. He usually liked dogs, but the terrier's wild barking had set his nerves on edge. In the awkward silence he and Gwen felt self-conscious. They could hear Frank's dog still barking outside. Larry asked, "So that's him, huh?"

"Yes, we grew up together," Gwen replied.

"He looks like a nice guy. What does Frank do?" Larry asked politely.

"He's the gamekeeper for your father's estate."

"Oh." Larry felt uncomfortable being reminded of the difference in rank between him and Gwen. Things weren't like this in America. A man and a woman simply fell in love. They didn't have to be matched according to social standing.

Frank returned without his dog. Larry once more offered his hand. Frank ignored it, his green eyes fixed on Larry's cane.

A hot blush rose to Larry's cheeks. He was only trying to be friendly. He half expected the man to bark like his nasty little dog. If Frank was going to be rude, it was perhaps better to leave. "Glad to know you, Andrews," Larry said formally. His long legs twitched with the urge to walk. "I . . . er . . . just came over to see that Gwen was all right. I guess I'd better be going now. Good-bye."

"Good-bye," Gwen said softly.

48

Frank did not reply. His angry eyes followed Larry out the door.

Gwen scolded, "Why were you so rude?"

"I'm sorry," Frank said, feeling a little silly. "I couldn't take my eyes off that cane of his. Be careful, Gwen, will you?"

"Careful?" Gwen asked. What was Frank talking about?

"He's been away for eighteen years, but he's still the son of Sir John Talbot," Frank explained lamely.

"Oh, I see. And I'm the daughter of Charles Conliffe, who merely owns the antique shop. Is that it?" Gwen asked. She had no more patience with the fine points of social order than Larry did. These were modern times, and she would be friends with whomever she chose. The sooner Frank got used to that, the better!

"Yes, that and . . . well . . . there's something very tragic about that man," Frank said thoughtfully. "I'm sure that nothing but harm will come to you through him."

CHAPTER 7
The Charm

That night the Gypsy camp was filled with the sounds of a noisy carnival. Crowds of villagers had come for the games, music, fortune-tellers, and fire-eaters. The men wore flat black hats and wide pants; the women, flowing skirts. Lanterns glowed like giant fireflies in the bare trees.

Frank and Gwen strolled past a crowd watching a Gypsy girl dance. Behind her a band played a lively tune on violins, tambourines, and accordions. Her bright skirt twirled around her bare stamping feet. The girl finished her dance to loud applause.

Frank asked, "Now, aren't you glad I brought you?"

Gwen nodded and her blue eyes shone. They smiled at each other, glad to be together.

Larry saw the happy couple, but quickly looked away. He nervously fingered his cane. All these people made him edgy; their happiness seemed to mock his sorrow. He was also angry that Gwen preferred the huntsman to him.

50

Frank said to Gwen, "There's Larry Talbot. Let's go and say hello, eh?"

She hesitated. "Well . . ."

"I just wanted to show you I'm not jealous," Frank confessed. Gwen smiled. Frank hurried after Larry, calling his name.

Larry tried to disappear into the noisy crowd. But he was a head taller than anyone else in the camp, and his large shoulders jostled the strolling villagers. He looked for a way to escape, but found none in the cheerful throng. He felt trapped.

Frank and Gwen caught up with him at a shooting gallery. Tin targets paraded at the back of the curtained booth. Several painted animals made of tin marched across a fake landscape. Others twirled around a rotating disk.

Larry politely tipped his hat to Gwen. He hoped his stiff smile hid the uncomfortable feeling he felt toward Frank.

Frank said casually, "We saw you walking along by yourself and thought you might like to join us."

"Well, thanks, but I was just on my way home," Larry said through clenched teeth. He felt hot and his clothes itched. He wanted more than anything to run away, but felt confined by good manners. He didn't want Gwen to be angry with him.

"Come on," Frank said. "We'll have some fun together." He waved a hand to indicate the shooting gallery and other games.

"Please do," Gwen urged. She wanted to see Larry smile again. She hoped the men could become friends.

Frank turned to the Gypsy running the booth. He tossed coins on the counter. "Two guns, please."

"Yes, sir," the man said, scooping the coins into an embroidered apron. He handed rifles to Frank and Larry.

Larry laid his cane on the counter. He aimed his rifle at the tin targets.

Frank smiled. "Let's see what you can do." He looked forward to besting his rival in this game of marksmanship. The young gamekeeper was, after all, a skilled hunter.

"All right," Larry agreed. He enjoyed hunting, too.

A short distance away, Sir John and Colonel Montford watched as Larry fired twice. The shots popped. With the ping of pellets on tin, a leopard and a bear fell.

Sir John spoke proudly. "He seems to be able to handle a rifle."

Larry took aim again and struck a small tin lion. Then a new target sprang up.

Larry looked along the rifle barrel. But when he saw the target, he could not pull the trigger. Disturbed, he lowered the gun. The painted wolf on the target seemed to stare back at him with human eyes.

Frank and Gwen watched, puzzled. Larry had been doing so well. "Go ahead and shoot before he bites you," Frank said playfully. Gwen laughed.

Larry's face distorted with effort. He aimed the gun determinedly. He closed his eyes and fired. The wolf did not fall.

"Bad luck," the gamekeeper said genially as he took careful aim. The gun popped and the wolf target flopped over. "See? Nothing to it. Care to try another one?"

THE WOLF MAN

Larry put his rifle down on the counter and picked up his hat and cane. He was overcome with strange emotions. His chest felt tight. His shirt stuck to his sweaty body. "No thanks. You win," he managed to say before hurrying away.

Larry's hasty departure worried Sir John. He turned to Colonel Montford and said, "He's unstrung from the long trip and that unfortunate accident the other night."

Larry's mind reeled. He felt prickly all over. Piercing voices and music echoed in his ears as he pawed through the thick crowds in the Gypsy camp. His nose was assaulted by strange smells.

He found himself before a huge black kettle bubbling over a campfire. A black horse was tied to a twisted tree close by. As if expecting him, the old Gypsy woman, Maleva, waved for Larry to come inside her tent. She said, "You've been a long while coming."

Larry stepped inside the canvas shelter. The air inside the tent was smoky from herbs steaming in a small cast-iron pot on the table. The choking reek of cooking and candles and strange potions made Larry want to tear open his shirt collar and run for a breath of fresh air. "I'm not buying anything," he told the old woman defiantly. There was something about her that he didn't like.

"And I'm not selling anything! I expected you sooner," she said mysteriously.

Larry looked at her lined face. "I remember you. That

night—and in the tomb."

"You killed the wolf!" Maleva said.

"There's no crime in that, is there?" Larry snarled.

"The wolf was Bela," Maleva said calmly.

"You think I don't know the difference between a wolf and a man?" Larry was furious. Here was another person telling him what he saw. They all thought he was crazy. They were wrong!

The old Gypsy woman continued, "Bela became a wolf and you killed him. A werewolf can be killed only with a silver bullet, or a silver knife—or a cane with a silver head."

"You're insane!" Larry barked. "I tell you, I killed a wolf—a plain, ordinary wolf!"

Maleva held up a chain with a charm on it. "Take this charm. It is the pentagram. It is the sign of the wolf! It can break the evil spell."

"Evil spell? Pentagram? Wolfsbane?" Larry raged. He'd had enough of this nonsense. He was sick of the whole nasty business. "I'm getting out of here!"

Maleva chanted, "Whoever is bitten by a werewolf—and lives—becomes a werewolf himself!"

"Aw, quit handing me that. You're just wasting your time," her visitor growled.

"The wolf bit you, didn't he?" Maleva asked.

"Yeah, he did!" Larry knew it was true, even if no one else believed him.

The old woman stepped up to him and put the charm around Larry's neck. "Wear this charm over your heart always!"

54

"All right, all right. I'll take it. What's it worth to you? I'll give you . . ." Larry fumbled in his pockets. His fingers felt thick and clumsy.

But Maleva did not want any money. Her black eyes pierced his. "Do you dare to show me the wound?" she asked.

"What?" Larry felt a chill run up his spine. But he unbuttoned his shirt so Maleva could see his chest. Where the wound should have been was a five-pointed star: the mark of the pentagram!

She lifted her sad eyes. "Go now, and heaven help you!"

Larry hastily buttoned his shirt, grabbed his hat and cane, and left. Maleva stared after him as he rushed out into the night. She saw the round moon hanging in the branches of the trees. She wrapped her shawl more tightly around her shoulders.

Puffing on his pipe, Colonel Montford watched Larry hurry through the carefree crowd. Sir John might not want to admit it, but something was wrong with Larry.

Maleva hurried to her fellow Gypsies, gathered around the campfire. She whispered to several, who went on to whisper to others, until the word spread like wildfire.

The Gypsies began folding their tents and packing their goods into painted wagons. They filled carpetbags and doused campfires, all at top speed. Booths snapped shut. The confused villagers milled about, wondering why the party was suddenly over.

Gwen bumped into Larry at the edge of the camp.

"I'm glad to see you!" he said. "But I thought you were with Frank."

"No, we had a quarrel and . . ." Gwen sighed.

"I'll take you home," Larry offered. He was eager for another chance to be alone with Gwen.

They walked into the woods. Moonlight sifted through branches, casting a net of shadows over the misty path.

"Quite a night, isn't it?" Larry asked.

Gwen glanced at him and noticed the metal star shining on his chest. "What's that?" she wondered.

"That's a charm. I just saw the old Gypsy woman. They give you quite a sales pitch, don't they?" Larry said, trying to sound normal. His skin felt tight and his shoes pinched.

"Let me see. A pentagram!" Gwen exclaimed.

"Yes. She said I was a werewolf." Larry laughed. What had seemed so ominous in the Gypsy's tent sounded ridiculous to him now. With the pretty girl beside him and the soft sighing of the cool breeze, just for a little while he wanted to forget the old woman's warning and all the ugliness that came with it.

Gwen said, "You can't believe that."

But perhaps he did. Larry felt so strange, and with all that had happened since he'd come home, anything seemed possible. He lifted the charm and put it around Gwen's neck. "I won't need this. I want you to have it. It'll protect you."

"Protect me? From what?"

Larry looked into her lovely blue eyes. "Me. Just in case." He leaned closer to Gwen. His face seemed enormous to her. She saw the moon reflected in his dark eyes.

She stepped away from him. "I never accept a present without giving something in return. Here's a penny."

But before Gwen could reach into her purse, Larry shook his head. "That's not enough," he said in a low, thick voice.

He moved closer as if to kiss Gwen. But a horse whinnied behind them, and Larry was startled by how loud it sounded. His ears were keenly aware of pots and pans clanging together, of wheels creaking, and of the irritating jingle of silver bells strung on wagons lurching between the trees. The air suddenly felt charged with panic. "All the Gypsies are leaving!" Larry cried out.

"I must go, too," Gwen said. She was frightened by Larry's mood and his wild expression. She hurried away.

"But, Gwen . . ." Larry called after her. He stopped a nearby Gypsy. "Hey, hey, hey! What's all the excitement?" Larry asked.

"There's a werewolf in camp!" the Gypsy cried. And without another word, he hurried away.

CHAPTER 8
The Wolf Man

Larry's scalp prickled. He felt as if every hair on his head was standing on end. His ears hurt from the shouts of the Gypsies, the cracking whips, and the rustle of leaves under his feet. He felt as if the world had suddenly started spinning faster and faster and he was all alone at the center.

Larry wriggled with a feverish itch. His skin tightened as if he were growing too large for his own body. His shirt gripped his chest like a straitjacket. His shoes were clumsy, painful prisons that tripped him as he ran frantically for home.

When he finally reached Talbot Castle, Larry gratefully slammed the heavy door behind him. The muscles in his hands knotted and squirmed. He looked down at his fingers—they seemed to have curved into claws. He ripped off his coat and shirt and looked at his bare arms. Every hair stood straight up. And even as he looked, the mottled skin sprouted more hair.

He yanked off his shoes and socks. Hair covered his ankles

and inched down his suddenly crooked feet.

Larry's heart raced with a terrible sense of inescapable doom. Air rushed in and out of his lungs. His ears rang with the sounds of the night. His body heaved with aches and twitches; bones groaned and cracked in unnatural contortions. The room whirled around him, and all the color drained from his sight.

The lights flickered. He felt as if his skull were splitting. His teeth wriggled in his jaw as they sprouted into giant fangs.

And then he didn't know anything anymore, except the urge to run free!

Now part wolf and part man, he loped along the mist-covered ground. His powerful legs bounded over roots and rocks. His furry chest expanded as it took in great gulps of forest air. He heard owls swooping through the night, and field mice squeaking over the leaves. His jaws parted in a ferocious howl of animal joy.

Now that he had escaped from the place that smelled of men and fire, he was ready to hunt. The change had made him hungry, and he smelled prey.

The Wolf Man snarled as he followed the scent to the lonely churchyard. Saliva dripped from his fangs.

A single lantern hung from the branch of a tree. It cast a glow on a tired gravedigger, Mr. Richardson. He put down his shovel when he heard howling in the woods. He struck a match on a nearby crumbling gravestone, its inscription long since weathered away. The night was becoming foggy, but certain things could still be seen: a weeping stone angel mourning the grave of a dearly beloved daughter, a Celtic cross that was tilted over the sunken grave of a knight.

Richardson was used to this silent, desolate place. His father and grandfather had dug their share of these graves. Tonight he worked late, preparing the earth to receive yet another body being laid to rest. This was the second grave he had dug today, and his back ached.

Richardson lit his pipe and nearly dropped the match when he again heard the shrill howling. The awful noise was now much closer, and it didn't sound like any dog he had ever heard. Richardson felt a clammy fear creep up into his wiry shoulders. The terrified man held his pipe in a trembling hand. He peered blindly into the fog.

Just beyond the lantern's faint circle of light, the gravedigger saw a pair of glowing eyes. They were peering at him from behind a thick tree. He heard a low growl, and then a shadowy form lurched directly at him. A scream choked in Richardson's throat. What he saw was more than a wolf; it was a nightmare!

The poor man didn't even have time to grab up his shovel, or say a prayer. The monster leapt at his neck. Man and beast fell wrestling into the open grave. Slashing fangs and powerful claws ripped and tore the warm, red life from Richardson's veins.

The last sound the dying gravedigger heard was the triumphant cry of a wolf.

The cry shattered the night and woke up the sleeping village. Through the fog, lights snapped on in windows everywhere. Sleepy people appeared in doorways on every street.

THE WOLF MAN

The old night watchman, Mr. Wykes, was walking these streets as usual. He came to a halt and called up to Officer Twiddle's window. "Did you hear that, Mr. Twiddle?"

"Of course I did, or I'd still be snug and warm in my bed," Twiddle griped. His heart thumped with fear.

"It sounded like a wild animal," said Mr. Phillips from the window next door.

"Maybe it's a beast that the Gypsies left behind," Wykes suggested.

Colonel Montford, the Chief Constable, had arrived in the street below Twiddle's window.

Mr. Wykes told him, "The howl seemed to come from the churchyard."

Montford looked up and called, "Don't stand there talking. Let's go and see!"

"All right," Twiddle said and reached for his trousers.

A search party followed Colonel Montford and Officer Twiddle to the deserted graveyard. Richardson's lamp sputtered above the little knot of men gathered around the open grave, where the unfortunate gravedigger lay sprawled in the dirt. Dr. Lloyd appeared like a ghost from the mist, his open coat flapping in the fog. "Good morning, Colonel," the doctor said.

"It could be a better one," Colonel Montford replied bitterly.

Dr. Lloyd crouched down to get a closer look at the body. "Richardson, the gravedigger, eh?"

A villager named Cotton answered, "Yes."

"Severed jugular," the doctor reported.

Colonel Montford studied the ground and said grimly, "Just the way Jenny Williams was killed."

"Yes," Dr. Lloyd agreed. "Find something?"

Colonel Montford mumbled. "Animal tracks. They belong to a wolf."

CHAPTER 9
Waking From a Nightmare

Larry woke up in his bed fully dressed. He was lying across the rumpled blankets. His body ached; his mouth was dry. Then, as he rubbed the last bit of heavy sleep from his eyes, he dimly recalled a most amazing dream.

He glanced down and saw that his bare feet were caked with mud. A trail of muddy prints was visible on the thick carpet. The prints close to his bed were those of human feet, but as they neared the windowsill, they became the pawprints of a gigantic wolf.

Larry fumbled with his shirt and fingered the mark of the pentagram on his chest. This was no dream! The legends he had scoffed at, those silly fairy tales, were real! He was seized with panic.

His breath came in ragged gasps. He frantically wiped at the muddy prints that marked his terrible secret. He brushed the dirt from the windowsill and was startled to see Colonel Montford on the lawn outside. The colonel, carrying a rifle, followed the trail of pawprints approaching the castle.

Larry flattened himself behind a heavy drape. What could he do? He hadn't meant to hurt anyone. He couldn't help himself. He could barely believe any of this was really happening. And right now his father's friend was hunting him, like a hound on the scent of a helpless hare.

Larry dressed hastily and hurried downstairs. Sir John greeted his son. "Ah, good morning, Larry. You're up early."

Larry stammered, "I h-heard people in the corridor. Is there anything wrong?" He dreaded the answer.

"Richardson, the gravedigger, was killed last night," said Sir John. Then he added, "The tracks lead up to this house."

"Footprints?" Larry asked.

"No. Animal tracks—a wolf!" Sir John exclaimed.

Larry pretended to be surprised. "A wolf! Where do you suppose a wolf came from?"

Sir John thought a moment, then said, "It might have escaped from a circus or a zoo."

"What is the story about a man turning into a wolf?" Larry asked. Inside his large body lurked the little boy who still believed his brilliant father had the answer to all questions. Maybe his father could find a cure!

"You mean—the werewolf?" Sir John asked. The great scholar was amused.

"Yes, sir," Larry said earnestly.

"It's an old legend," Sir John said in the tone he used in his college lectures. "You'll find something like it in the folklore of nearly every nation."

Sir John opened a thick book. Larry peered over his shoulder. On the page it said:

lycanthropy \li-`kan-thre-pē\ n: 1. a delusion that one has become a wolf. 2: taking on the form and characteristics of a wolf through witchcraft or magic.

Larry slumped down to sit on the corner of a table.

Sir John continued. "The scientific name is *lykanthropia*. But it's more commonly known as werewolfism, a disease of the mind in which human beings imagine they become wolfmen."

"It's all Greek to me," Larry confessed. He always felt dumb around his learned father.

"It *is* Greek!" Sir John said with a smile. "Lycanthropy is a technical expression for something very simple—the good and evil in every man's soul." He paced thoughtfully. "In this case the evil is believed to take the shape of an animal."

Larry jumped up, nearly hysterical. "I can figure out almost anything if you give me electric current and tubes and wires. I can do anything with my hands—but this is something you can't even touch . . ."

"What's the matter with you, Larry?" asked Sir John. His son had been acting strangely ever since that unfortunate business in the marsh.

"Nothing, nothing, sir." Larry made an effort to appear calm.

"But . . . do you believe these legends?"

The older man coolly considered the question. "Larry, to some people life is very simple. They decide, 'This is good; that is bad. This is wrong; that is right.' There are no shadings of grays—things are either black or white."

Larry nodded. "Paul Montford."

"Exactly," Sir John said with a wry smile. "Now, others of us find that good, bad, right, wrong are many-sided, complex things."

Larry frowned, thoughtful. He wanted answers, but his father preferred to talk in theories.

Sir John lectured on. "We try to see every side, and the more we see, the less sure we are. Now, you ask me if I believe a man can become a wolf."

Larry nodded eagerly. At last his father was coming to the point!

"If you mean, can a man take on the physical characteristics of an animal—no! It's fantastic!" Sir John declared.

Larry's heart sank. If his father's great mind could not grasp the dreadful truth, what hope did he have of finding a solution?

Sir John's voice took on a tone of deep conviction. "However, I do believe that almost anything can happen to a man in his own mind."

Larry briefly wondered if he were going mad. But madness did not leave mud on your windowsill. No, worse than madness, this terrible change was real!

Church bells tolled in the village. The footman came into the study. "Time for church," he said.

THE WOLF MAN

Sir John nodded. "You know, Larry, a belief in the hereafter is a very healthy thing to have, with all the doubts man is prey to these days." Sir John took his hat from the footman. Larry took his hat, too. Maybe he would find peace in the church.

Outside the church the congregation huddled together on the sagging steps. Cars and carriages brought worshippers to the old stone chapel. The bells rang solemnly.

Mr. Wykes sighed. "Ah, last night it caught up with Richardson."

Mr. Phillips nodded sadly and hunched deeper inside his dark wool coat. "Many's the grave he dug for others—now they're digging one for him."

Miss Bally, a stout, elderly villager, added her shrill voice to the discussion. "I don't dare open my door anymore for fear of that beast."

Jenny's mother, Mrs. Williams, bleated, "That beast! Has anybody ever seen it? I don't believe it even exists!" She paused and the bells tolled again. "Very strange that there were no murders here before Larry Talbot arrived. I think—"

Mr. Twiddle interrupted her. "Hold your tongue, Mrs. Williams! Do you know that's slander?"

Mrs. Williams didn't care. "I know what I know! You didn't see the way he looked at me in Conliffe's shop—like a wild animal with murder in his eyes!"

Mr. Phillips hushed the hysterical woman. "Shh! Here he comes."

The Talbots arrived in the same dark limousine that had brought Larry home. The young man stood by the car, staring up at the sharp steeple that pierced the sky. Moss and ivy crawled over the old stones of the church; stale water dripped from the slate roof. Hideous gargoyles leered down with mocking stone smiles. Larry cringed under the carved monsters' sightless gaze.

Sir John greeted people and followed the flock up the wide steps. Larry forced himself to follow. Near the large double door, they met Charles Conliffe and Gwen.

Sir John and the shopkeeper exchanged pleasantries.

Gwen said softly, "How are you, Larry?" She could not help being worried by the haunted look in his dark eyes.

"Fine, thank you," Larry answered mechanically. The organ music drifting through the open church doors sounded sour in his ears.

Mr. Conliffe urged Gwen inside. Sir John climbed the steps with a brisk step. Larry followed reluctantly.

By this time the rest of the congregation had been seated. Sir John quickly took his place in the first pew. Larry lingered at the back of the church near the door. The last few stragglers brushed past him.

All at once the villagers turned to look at Larry. He felt as if he were standing before them naked. Their faces were as strange and cold as the gargoyles'. These were not the friendly villagers his father spoke of with such calm affection. These people hated him. They hunted him. They wanted him dead.

THE WOLF MAN

Dr. Lloyd studied the young man's troubled face. Colonel Montford also stared at Larry with suspicion. Even Sir John turned around to look at his son. He wondered what everyone thought of Larry's strange actions.

Larry's legs would not obey his mind. His will could not overcome some invisible barrier that prevented him from entering the church. With a whimpering moan, he finally turned and fled.

CHAPTER 10
Tracks and Traps

That afternoon Colonel Montford sat at the desk in the library at Talbot Castle. He bent to examine a white plaster cast of a huge pawprint. Sir John and Dr. Lloyd looked over his shoulder. Frank Andrews relaxed on the arm of a couch near the others.

Montford said, "I think I'll send this cast of the animal's tracks to the experts at Scotland Yard."

Sir John asked, "Why? They'll laugh at you. There's no question about it. It's a wolf."

Frank spoke up. "Bigger than any wolf I've ever seen. He's probably hiding in the woods somewhere. How about traps?"

Dr. Lloyd said, "We've got to do something before the people of the town become completely hysterical."

Colonel Montford stood and stretched. "Yes, all this muttering about werewolves."

Larry walked into the room and they all looked up. For a

dizzy moment Larry felt as if he stood frozen at the church door again. He felt as if he did not belong in this roomful of men.

"Come in, Larry. We're discussing the wolf that seems to be roaming the countryside," his father said.

Larry hesitated. He felt everyone's eyes on him. He wondered what they had said about his running out of the church.

Frank turned to Larry. "You saw the wolf. What's he like? Is he as huge as these tracks would indicate?"

So at last they believed there was a wolf. How long would it take before they would believe the wolf was also a man? "It isn't a wolf," Larry said. "It's a werewolf!"

"A werewolf!" Frank was flabbergasted. Larry Talbot, with his American ways, was the last person he thought would believe in superstitions.

Colonel Montford laughed. "Maybe he's right. Let's have a hunt and drive it out. It would be a valuable addition to anybody's collection. Just imagine having a stuffed werewolf staring at you from the wall."

"I wouldn't joke about it, Paul," Dr. Lloyd cautioned.

Larry approached the doctor. He came closer. His brown eyes were glowing with passion. "Do you believe in werewolves?"

The doctor was taken aback. Was young Talbot truly insane? Dr. Lloyd humored him. "Why, I believe that a man lost in the mazes of his mind may imagine that he's anything. Scientists have found many examples of the mind's power over the body. The case of the stigmata appearing on the skin of zealots . . ."

Larry had heard about stigmata—the marks of the Cross that

appeared on the hands and feet of some devout Christians.

Sir John frowned. Church was all well and good, but some people took it too far. He snorted. "Stigmata are just a form of self-hypnosis."

Larry's dark eyes searched the doctor's face. "But if a man isn't even thinking about the thing—isn't interested in it—how could he hypnotize himself with it?"

Dr. Lloyd pondered. "It might be a case of mental suggestion, plus mass hypnotism."

"You mean a man could be influenced by the people around him?" Larry thought of all the people who had recited that dreadful poem to him.

"Yes," Dr. Lloyd confirmed.

Sir John chided, "Oh, come now, Doctor, you're allowing your science to run away with your common sense." He did not want anyone feeding Larry's already strange beliefs. What would people think if the last Talbot went about spouting Gypsy nonsense and jumping at every full moon?

Frank asked, "Have you ever met a werewolf?"

"Not that I know of," Dr. Lloyd replied.

Larry bent toward him eagerly. "Doctor, can these sick people be cured?"

Colonel Montford stood before the fireplace, knocking the ashes from his pipe. He sneered, "An asylum is the only safe place for them."

The doctor did not agree. "Any disease of the mind can be cured with the cooperation of the patient."

Frank stood and straightened his coat. "Well, while you gentlemen are figuring it out scientifically, I think I'll go and set a few traps," he said, starting to walk out of the room.

Colonel Montford appreciated a man of action. "I'll help you," he said. Frank and Montford made their way to the door. "We may not catch anything more than a diseased mind, but even that may be interesting," the colonel added with a sly smile.

Larry ignored them and turned to Dr. Lloyd. "I've got to talk to you."

The doctor replied, "Later on. Now I want you to go and get some rest."

"Go on, Larry." Sir John dismissed his son as if Larry were still a child. Larry hesitated, then lumbered out.

Once he was gone, Dr. Lloyd turned to Sir John. "*You're* the one I want to talk to."

"I didn't like what you said to Larry about mass hypnotism," Sir John said loftily.

"Sir John, your son is a sick man," Dr. Lloyd stated. "He's received a shock that has caused definite psychic maladjustment. You must send him away from this village!"

Sir John stood with his hands in his pockets, his mind fixed. The last Talbot would never leave this castle. "You're talking like a witch doctor. If my son is ill, the best place for him is in his own home, proving his innocence."

"Does the prestige of the family name mean more to you than your son's health?" Dr. Lloyd asked bitterly. He knew Sir John was a proud and stubborn man.

"Nonsense!" Sir John exclaimed. "The only way for Larry to get cured is for him to stay here and fight his way out of this."

"And I tell you, the shock is too much for him in his present state," the doctor asserted. He was sure Larry was headed toward a nervous breakdown.

Sir John was adamant. "Listen to me. Five generations of Talbots have not been affected by this village. That boy stays here!"

"Very well." Dr. Lloyd knew better than to argue with Sir John when his mind was made up. The doctor took his hat and coat. "We'll see how he is in the morning."

Meanwhile, deep in the forest, Frank and Colonel Montford directed the placement of traps. Volunteers from the village covered the lethal steel jaws with dead leaves, which made the perfect camouflage. The sharp metal spikes would spring shut at the slightest step. Each trap was linked by a sturdy chain to a heavy stake driven into the ground.

They had spent the better part of the evening laying many traps all over the woods. Anything smaller than an elephant would be held until an armed huntsman arrived.

Mr. Wykes put his shovel on a cart loaded with tools. "Done, sir."

Frank asked, "The last one, eh?"

Montford was satisfied with the preparations. "That ought to hold him," he said.

CHAPTER 11
Steel Jaws

When the full moon climbed again, the Wolf Man stalked among dim and shadowy trees. His keen senses were on the alert for prey. One of his hairy feet stepped onto a pile of leaves. Something suddenly snapped shut! The Wolf Man howled with pain, snarled, and thrashed on the forest floor. His vision went red with rage and agony. All his great strength was useless against these strange metal jaws. And now he could hear the baying of hounds!

The Wolf Man crawled away from that dreadful sound. He would be helpless before a pack of dogs. He had to get away. Snarling and heaving, he finally wrenched the anchoring stake out of the ground. The smell of man and dog filled his nostrils. He saw lights bobbing in the mist.

He could not stand on his bleeding paw, clamped in those cruel jaws. He fell and crawled through a wide pool of brackish marsh water. Then the Wolf Man hid behind a fallen tree.

The lights and men and horrible dogs neared the pool. He

could not understand their noises, but he knew they were hunting him!

Mr. Wykes looked at the confused pack of circling hounds. He could see that the leaves were disturbed. Something large had passed through, but the dogs could not follow its scent through water. "They've lost the trail, sir," he reported.

Frank Andrews snapped, "He can't have disappeared into thin air."

Colonel Montford instructed, "Take Phillips and work around the marsh. See if you can pick up the trail down there."

Mr. Phillips called to some other villagers, "Come on, men."

On the other side of the marsh, Maleva found the Wolf Man lying senseless on the soggy ground. The old woman's instinct had told her to break away from the Gypsy caravan and return to this cursed forest.

She stepped down from her cart and knelt over the shivering Wolf Man. She waved her weathered hands over him, muttering Gypsy spells. Then her sad voice mourned, " 'The way you walk is thorny, through no fault of your own. But as the rain enters the soil, the river enters the sea, so tears run to a predestined end. . . .' "

The bloody paw clamped in the trap writhed and straightened. The fur fell away, and in its place was human skin.

"Find peace for a moment, my son," Maleva said.

Larry's head whipped restlessly back and forth. He opened his eyes and saw the old Gypsy woman kneeling beside him. "What are you doing here?" he moaned.

Maleva said quietly, "I came to help you."

Larry felt the terrible pain in his foot, then leaves under his back and cold, damp marsh air. "Where am I?" he asked. "What happened?"

Maleva pulled herself up on creaky knees. Her gnarled fingers struggled to open the steel jaws. "You are caught in a trap," she said, grunting with effort.

"Let me do that!" Larry said. But even he could not open the cold, unyielding steel.

The dogs bayed and barked. Lights and shadows flitted through the nearby trees. The hunters and their hounds thrashed through the underbrush.

"Hurry! The dogs! They are hunting you!" Maleva warned.

With desperate strength, Larry forced open the trap. He limped away as fast as he could.

A voice called, "Hello! Stop! Come here! You!"

Mr. Wykes and Mr. Phillips stopped by a tree. Their dogs strained toward Larry as he lurched past.

"It's Master Larry!" Wykes gasped. "What are you doing here, sir?"

Larry managed a reply. "The same thing that you are, of course—hunting." He walked on without stopping.

Colonel Montford appeared out of the mist. "I heard you talking to someone," he said.

"Master Larry," Wykes reported.

"All right, go along." Colonel Montford held his lantern high. He was surprised to see Larry Talbot disappear into the fog. He was certain that Sir John's son had not been one of the hunting party.

CHAPTER 12
The Hand of Fate

Lighted windows glowed above the foggy village street like floating ghosts in a dream. Larry hurried painfully down the damp cobblestones until he came to Charles Conliffe's antique shop. He tossed pebbles at the upper window where he had first seen Gwen.

The rocks rattled against the glass. Larry fidgeted. He didn't know how long Maleva's spell would keep him human.

The window swung open and Gwen's sleepy face leaned out. Larry could not speak and only spread his hands helplessly. His dark eyes stared at her, full of need. His hair was a mess of tangles and leaves. His clothes were ripped and wrinkled. Blood dribbled from his bare ankle. But the wound was already closing with unnatural speed.

Larry watched a single lamp make its way downstairs. He wished Gwen would hurry. He looked up and down the quiet street, ears alert for the slightest sound. When the shop bell jangled, he jumped.

Gwen whispered, "Larry!" She ushered him into the shop.

"I'm going away," Larry said mournfully. He had to see her one last time, to say good-bye.

"Away? Why?" Gwen was not quite awake.

Larry groaned. "I have to go! I can't stay here."

Gwen rushed to him, clinging to his broad chest. "Let me go with you! I'll fetch a few things and be back in a minute."

Larry panicked. "No! I'm going alone!"

"But I can help you!" Gwen protested.

"Do you want to run away with a murderer?" Larry asked. He had already caused Gwen enough trouble. How could he ask her to go away with a man who became a savage wolf?

"You know you're not!" Gwen cried.

Larry's face twisted with pain. "I killed Bela! I killed Richardson! If I stay here any longer, who knows what'll happen? I might even . . ."

Gwen pleaded with him. "Please. I still have the charm you gave me. Remember?"

"I know, but I'm afraid!" Larry took her small hands in his and stared at the upturned palms. He saw the five-pointed star of the pentagram etched in her soft skin. His body twitched and quivered with animal hunger, which faded with the star.

Gwen watched his anguished face. "What is it?"

Larry broke away from her, horrified. "Your hand!"

Just then Mr. Conliffe came downstairs. Gwen was at the point of tears. She looked at her hand, "I can't see anything."

Mr. Conliffe said sternly, "Mr. Talbot!"

Gwen mustered her courage and announced, "Father, I'm going with Larry."

Larry felt his skin crawl with the first itching pain of the change. He cried out, "No! It's no use!" He whirled and rushed out the door, slamming it behind him with a furious jangling of the shop bell.

Mr. Conliffe wrapped his arms around his sobbing daughter.

In Talbot Castle, Sir John was surprised to see his son at the front door. "Going out, Larry?"

"Father, I've got to get away from here. Bela the Gypsy was a werewolf. I killed him with that silver cane," Larry blurted out. He opened his shirt. "I was bitten. Look—the pentagram!"

Sir John studied the five-pointed star. He felt a chill of fear. Like any Welshman, he knew what the mark meant. But he could not believe his own son had become a monster. "That scar could be made by any animal," Sir John scoffed.

Larry shook his head miserably. "It's the sign of the werewolf. They say he can see it in the palm of his next victim."

Sir John refused to be swayed. "It's hard to believe."

"I saw it—tonight, in Gwen's hand!" his son cried.

"Larry! Larry! How can I help you get rid of this fear—this mental quagmire you've got yourself into? What can I say to you?" Sir John pleaded. How could he make things right?

"You don't understand," Larry said impatiently. "You think I'm insane." Hounds howled and barked outside the stone walls.

Larry looked around in fear. "What's that?"

"That's Paul Montford and the men," his father stated. "They caught nothing in their traps, so now they're going to hunt the wolf."

Larry wasn't listening. He shuddered under a wave of cramps and convulsions, then rushed upstairs, with Sir John at his heels. The dogs barked louder, drawing ever closer to their prey. Larry whimpered, "They're hunting me!"

"Stop it, Larry! Stop it! You can't run away!" Sir John shouted.

"That's what she said," Larry muttered. His mind raced with desperation. He was trapped!

"Who?" Sir John wondered. His son was raving!

"The Gypsy woman!"

Now Sir John was angry. At last he knew whom to blame for his son's condition. "The Gypsy woman? Now you're getting to the bottom of this. She's been filling your mind with gibberish—talk of werewolves and pentagrams! You're not a child, Larry. You're a grown man, and yet you believe in the superstitions of a Gypsy woman!"

"But the scar, the footprints in my room!" Larry pointed to the clotted blood on his ankle. The wound itself was now only a faint scar. "Look, Father. I was caught in a trap tonight. I don't know how I got there. The old Gypsy woman helped me get away—and now they're all hunting me!'

Sir John did not even look at his son's leg. "Listen to me. You are Lawrence Talbot. This is Talbot Castle. You believe those men can come in here and take you out?" Sir John would never let anyone take his poor, deluded son from their ancestral home. This stone castle was a fortress!

"I'll go out to them. I can't help myself!" Larry whimpered.

But Sir John had a plan.

He took Larry up to his bedroom and strapped him into a large chair. While Sir John did this, Larry began to feel his skin crawling and his ears ringing. Through his bedroom window, he saw men and dogs circling the lawn in the bright moonlight. His eyesight had already lost the sense of color. He could now see only in black and white.

"There! You're tied in the chair—all the windows are locked," Sir John said. "I'll bolt the door so that nothing can get in or out. Now you'll see that this evil thing you've conjured up is only in your mind."

Roberts, the butler, called out, "Sir John! Colonel Montford and the men are waiting for you and Master Larry."

For an instant Sir John felt the same panic as his son. "I'm coming!" he called, determined to face the danger as a true Talbot.

Larry was afraid and struggled with the ropes. "But you're going to stay with me, aren't you?" If his father would only stay, maybe he could hold back the change.

Sir John said, "No, I've got to go, Larry. We'll settle this thing tonight."

Larry looked up at his father and cried, "Dad!"

"What is it?" Sir John asked impatiently.

THE WOLF MAN

"Take the cane with you," Larry begged.

Sir John was thoughtful. "What do I want with the cane?"

Larry pleaded, "Please, just take it with you. Please!"

"All right." Sir John picked up the silver-topped cane and left the room.

Larry turned his tortured gaze to look out the window. The full moon's round, glowing face seemed to laugh at his pain. He bowed his head as the change wracked his body.

CHAPTER 13
A Fateful End

"He should come right across through here," Colonel Montford said confidently. He and Frank Andrews and Dr. Lloyd crouched on a platform in the branches of a tree that stood near a clearing in the forest. From the raised platform, the hunters could safely shoot at the wolf. Other men were fanned out in a circle, beating the bush to drive the beast toward the platform.

"The men should drive it this way," Frank agreed. He checked his rifle again, anxious for the hunt to be over.

Sir John crossed the clearing. He carried the wolf's-head cane. Dr. Lloyd bent down to speak to him. "Did you give your son the sleeping pill?"

"No!"

Dr. Lloyd was frustrated by the stubborn Sir John. So many more patients could get well if they only listened to their doctors! "I wanted him to sleep through all this hullabaloo," Dr.

Lloyd explained.

"And I want him cured—tonight," Sir John countered. "By morning he'll have conclusive proof that it was all in his mind."

The doctor leaned on his rifle, worried. "What did you do?"

"Strapped him to a chair, turned him to the window so he can see something of the hunt," Sir John replied.

"I hope you won't be sorry," Dr. Lloyd said, but his heart felt heavy.

Montford heard something in the woods. "Dr. Lloyd!" he whispered.

The doctor and Sir John looked among the trees. Dr. Lloyd stood up and readied his rifle. Sir John did not want to witness the kill. Even killing an animal was too savage an act for the scholar. He would leave the hunters to their grim job and return to Talbot Castle. The doctor's words disturbed him. Sir John was anxious to check on Larry.

A sound from out of the darkness startled him. The old Gypsy woman sat like a ragged vulture on her cart. In the weak light of its hanging lantern, her wrinkled face seemed like a hideous mask. "You're not frightened, are you, Sir John?"

He looked at her with disgust. "Frightened? Of what?" She was just a dirty old busybody.

"Of the night," Maleva taunted.

"Rubbish! You startled me," Sir John said forcefully.

The old Gypsy smiled nastily. "Don't be startled, Sir John.

You have the silver cane for protection."

He glanced at the cane, then walked briskly toward the cart. Shadows from the branches looked like spiders' webs across her lined face. "Who are you?" he demanded.

"Hasn't your son told you?" Maleva asked.

Sir John frowned. "You're the Gypsy woman who's been filling his mind with this werewolf nonsense."

"Nonsense?" Maleva asked.

"Yes. You've been preying on his innocence with your witches' tales," Sir John accused.

"But you think you've helped him, don't you, Sir John?" Maleva teased. "You don't believe the witches' tales, do you?"

"Not for a minute."

Maleva's dark eyes glowed with knowledge. "Then, where were you going, Sir John? Why aren't you back there at the shooting stand?"

"I was . . ." He could not think of a good reply.

"Were you hurrying back to the castle? Did you have a moment's doubt? Were you hurrying to make sure he's all right?"

Sir John blustered, "I wanted to be with my son. I was going to . . ."

Gunshots echoed like thunder! They both listened, trying to be sure of the direction. Maleva watched Sir John's face.

"Yes, Sir John, you were going . . ." she prompted.

Sir John bolted into the trees. The calm scholar's determination vanished, leaving only a frightened father.

"Hurry, Sir John, hurry!" Maleva called after him.

"Come around this way, men!" Colonel Montford shouted to the men. "Swing out to the right there and come through again!"

The men hastened to obey the colonel's command, and they beat the bushes harder.

Frank Andrews added, "Wykes—you and Phillips take charge!"

The forest swarmed with restless dogs, armed men, and flaming torches.

Colonel Montford was confused. "I could have sworn I hit him dead on."

"I thought I did, too," said Frank, who was equally puzzled. "These heavy-caliber rifles should have dropped the beast."

"Have you forgotten it takes a silver bullet to kill a werewolf?" Dr. Lloyd asked. In the dark night the tales of his childhood came back to him. He had seen the bullets strike the animal's hide. It should have died!

"Have you seen Larry?" Gwen found Maleva in her pony cart near a thick oak tree. Overwhelmed with concern, Gwen had been to Talbot Castle, but the butler had turned her away. She had to see Larry!

Maleva warned, "Don't go through the woods."

"Why?" Gwen wondered.

The Gypsy looked off into the darkness. "Listen! The hunt is on!"

"But I want to help him," Gwen said.

"You'd better come with me," Maleva suggested.

Gwen grew more anxious. "No! I've got to find him!"

"Come with me—or he will find *you!*" the Gypsy warned in a voice laden with doom. Gwen panicked and ran away.

From behind that very oak tree, the Wolf Man watched, snarling. He had easily snapped the weak strands holding him prisoner in Talbot Castle. The hunters had shot at him, but their bullets had only hurt his ears. He was more afraid of their barking dogs that reeked with the smell of man. He knew they were trying to harm him.

The Wolf Man spotted a fleeing girl and loped after her.

Sir John also ran, puffing and swatting branches with the heavy cane. He saw lanterns swaying in the fog. Colonel Montford's men searched among the barren trees and bushes. They did not see the cunning monster tracking the hunters at the same time they were tracking him.

Gwen stopped to catch her breath. All around she saw the lights and heard the cries of dogs and hunters. She was startled to see a manlike shape detach itself from a scarred tree trunk. At first she thought it was a hunter. But then the moonlight fell on the monster's horrible snout and gleaming fangs!

With a bloodcurdling howl the Wolf Man lunged at Gwen. Her scream split the night.

88

THE WOLF MAN

Frank heard Gwen's scream and leapt from the shooting platform. He charged through the woods with his gun.

Sir John also heard the scream, and stood frozen for an instant when he saw the huge, hairy hulk holding the helpless girl. The monstrous yellow eyes fixed on Sir John. The Wolf Man dropped his prey and snarled.

Gwen's eyes flickered open. She struggled to her feet and ran into the woods.

Sir John advanced on the crazed creature. The beast tensed for the spring, with foaming lips drawn back in a hideous growl that raised the hair on Sir John's neck. He lifted the silver-headed cane.

The Wolf Man leapt, and Sir John struck with all his might. Man and beast rolled among the crackling leaves in mortal combat. Claws shredded Sir John's coat. The slavering fangs sought his throat. But Sir John raised the silver-headed cane and struck again and again, until the Wolf Man lay still.

Sir John leaned against the tree, exhausted. He stared down at the creature stretched on the blood-splashed leaves. Only then did he notice the Gypsy in her cart. The old crone climbed down to kneel beside the beast's body. She took its front paws in her own gnarled hands.

Maleva whispered, " 'The way you walked was thorny, through no fault of your own. . . .' "

As his mind cleared, Sir John saw that the beast wore Larry's clothes. It couldn't be! No! His mind fought the truth as his body had fought the Wolf Man.

Maleva droned on, " 'But as the rain enters the soil, the river enters the sea, so tears run to a predestined end.' "

Sir John watched fascinated, horrified, as the snout became a mouth, fangs receded into teeth, hair vanished from the great barrel chest, and the crooked claws straightened into hands.

" 'Your suffering is all over. Now you will find peace in eternity,' " Maleva said solemnly. She climbed onto her rickety cart and rolled off into the forest.

Sir John stood transfixed. He could not deny his own eyes. His son Larry lay beneath the tree, killed by the silver-headed cane.

Through the woods, members of the search party were running toward the tragic scene. Frank came upon Gwen, who was dazed and frightened. He held her tightly. "Are you all right?" he asked. She nodded, feeling safe in his arms, and they walked toward the others.

Moments later, Colonel Montford and the hunters found the grief-stricken Sir John, crouched beside Larry's battered body. Gwen gasped and covered her face with her hands. Dr. Lloyd dropped to his knees and quickly determined that Larry was dead. Though his bones were broken and his flesh was bloody, Larry's face wore a gentle, peaceful smile. Death had released him from the terrible curse.

Colonel Montford looked at the body, then at Sir John's pale, weary face. Montford knew his old friend's hopes were shattered. He could at least give Sir John his dignity.

"The wolf must have attacked Gwen, and Larry came to her rescue," he said at last. "I'm sorry, Sir John."

Gwen took her hands from her eyes and tried to remember what had really happened. Suddenly all of her fear vanished, and her heart filled with grief. Her eyes filled with tears as she once again remembered the ancient poem:

> One werewolf is free of the dreadful curse.
> But others still prowl the moonlight.
> If you walk through lonely woods at night,
> And the autumn moon is bright,
> Remember what the Gypsy said,
> And beware the wolfsbane white.
> But most of all, my friend,
> Beware the Wolf Man's bite!